SUPERBU HOMECOMING

The emotional story of a family and their dog (inspired by true events)

Debarshi Kanjilal

Novellaman.com

Copyright © 2020 Debarshi Kanjilal

This is a work of fiction that was inspired by true events. Although the basic ideas presented in this book come from real life, the names, characters, events, locales, and incidents have been altered or exaggerated for creative or dramatic purposes and have been used in a fictitious manner.

*To all those people who have been
transformed by the love of a dog.*

COLLABORATORS

Editing

Debdatta Purkayastha

Cover Design

Praful Jadhav

Beta Reading

Abantika Bose

Debdatta Purkayastha

Pubali Kanjilal

Nayan Basu

Vrushali Tillu

I'M GRATEFUL

- ✓ To dogs around the world who love us even when we are unable to love ourselves
- ✓ To all the families who gave a dog their heart, not just their home
- ✓ To my family, who continue to choose kindness every day, even when they do not have the guiding light of their beloved dog
- ✓ To the three girls who coerced me into thanking them in my next book but actually deserve my gratitude more than they realize
- ✓ To Buzo, the dog who forever changed me as a human being, as much in life as after

BEFORE WE BEGIN

It perhaps goes without saying, SuperBu is based on the life of my own dachshund dog, Buzo. The little time that my family and I got to spend with her was probably the most glued-together we ever were as a family. For our family, Bu was nothing short of a superhero who united us with her love and SuperBu is my attempt at making her story live on. Homecoming is the first novella in the Adventures of SuperBu series.

Not every event in this story is accurate to what happened with Buzo, but I tried to capture the gamut of emotions that the people involved experienced during the events that inspired this story.

This is not a children's book or a fairy tale. This book is not all about that fuzzy feeling that you get from stories about dogs. It explores a wide range of emotions and is perhaps best categorized as drama.

If you are looking for a book that'll keep you continuously smiling and laughing by through the antics of an adorable puppy, this is perhaps not the book for you.

So, now that you know what not to expect, let's talk about what you can expect from this book. Have you or someone you know ever felt like something is missing in your life and getting a dog could help you fill a void? Did you, or an acquaintance of yours, end up actually getting that dog? Did you and your dog figure out how to navigate through life together? This is the story of that dog, or a dog like that one. But more importantly, this is the story of that version of you, or that acquaintance of yours, who decided to act and bring home that dog, or of people like you who went through similar experiences in life.

If you have ever felt like you needed to be loved a little more than you are, I hope that this story tells you exactly how to find that love.

But before we begin, let me take a moment to request you to give a home to a homeless dog or contribute to projects dedicated to stray animals. At the end of this book, I will offer you a simple way to show your support to stray dogs.

Alright, let's begin!

***

CONTENTS

Title Page
Copyright
Dedication
Collaborators
I'm Grateful
Before We Begin

The Wait Ends Here	1
What's in a Name	18
All Good Things Must End	23
People Say Things	33
Isolation	43
The Plight of the Hapless	56
The Strength of Will	74
Family	80
Thank You for Reading...	95
The Buzoland Project	99

About The Author 101

THE WAIT ENDS HERE

The lazy young lad who would sleep through a freaking earthquake suddenly didn't need anyone to wake him up. It was a special Sunday morning in September.

Ajay was up at five in the morning. Not once did he hit the snooze button on the alarm clock. He did not sleep through the ringing alarm until someone else in the house got perturbed enough to shake him awake. He heard the alarm within the first few seconds of it going off. He woke up and switched off the alarm, so as not to wake the rest of the family. He did not lie back down over the scattered sheets on his bed like he usually would on any other day.

He got up, headed to the bathroom, freshened up, brushed his teeth, came back out, changed into an ironed, royal blue t-shirt and his grey jeans, and he sat down on the edge of the bed, yet to be made, posture annoyingly better than how he usually sat, and waited. He did not have to get up that early; there wasn't an exam to get to, no lectures at college that he feared he would be arriving late for, no potential girlfriend who had invited him to meet somewhere for a breakfast date.

It was a Sunday, but Ajay was ready and all dressed up to hit the city by 5:30 in the morning. Yet, this was only the second most unusual thing about this day, because this was also the day that the Bera family had finally agreed to bring home a dog.

Ajay had been dreaming about this day since he was eight; since the day that his mother had refused to adopt one of the puppies that her husband Ajit's colleague was willing to let them keep. It had been twelve years now that Ajay had been trying to coerce her into getting a puppy home and his mother, Barnali, had finally given in to his pestering, only earlier in the week. The window of opportunity was small. Barnali could, potentially, change her mind any minute. And that meant that in two days, Ajay went to the local vet, found out about a guy who had a lot of dogs and sold the puppies, and contacted him. Ajay made a list of the types of puppies he could get, learned how much of each type would cost, and chewed on how soon he could get one home.

Twelve years ago, Ajay had decided in his mind that he would get two puppies when he got the chance. One would be a German Shepherd Dog and another a Labrador or a Golden Retriever. If it, for unavoidable reasons, had to be just one puppy at a time, the first one would have to be the GSD. In his mind, Ajay had the names for both his dogs figured out already. But he did not consider all the hiccups that would come with it, when the opportunity presented itself.

A German Shepherd would cost more money than Ajit could spend, so he convinced Ajay that a German Shepherd would be too much upkeep for Ajay in how much exercise it would have to get to stay healthy. Ajit convinced Ajay that a German Shepherd Dog was likely to get depressed if it stayed inside the house most of the time. Ajit said a dachshund would be perfect for the house because he had one when he was a child, and he had never seen a creature more intelligent than that. And it had to be a female because the bitches are usually smarter than the dogs. Ajay believed his father. He was naïve like that. He generally believed what people said to him.

Not once did Ajay think about breeding practices when he met the guy brokering the sale of the puppy. He just accepted that the guy sold off the puppies if and when his dogs gave birth to a litter because, if not, raising those many dogs would become overwhelming for one family in very little time.

But Ajay was excited about the day ahead of him. He had only to meet the broker at 9 AM, but he sat still at the edge of the bed, with his spine straighter than ever, until 6 AM, when Barnali woke up and walked in looking to wake Ajay up.

"Yes, today is a good day to get ready at 6 AM, and the days of your exams are good days to sleep till nine after playing games and watching indecent videos on your phone till four in the morning," she said.

Ajay didn't care. He was happy that morning. Happier than that time he scored 24 unbeaten runs in a local cricket match and got a little six-inch trophy for his efforts. Happier than the time he scored a goal in that 3-on-3 football match at college that six guys cut class to play. Happier than when Ajit didn't drive him out of the house nor beat him to a pulp with his belt upon learning that he had failed two subjects in his first semester in college.

"Of course, nobody cares about what I want, anyway," Barnali continued. "There was only one thing I ever expected from my marriage, that I wouldn't have to live in a house where there would be dog hair and dog shit lying around everywhere."

That wasn't necessarily true. She expected a lot of other things from her husband. She had been dreaming about all the things that her would-be husband would give her since she was a teenage girl. Undying love, undivided attention, unrealistic longing, unending means, and a long, white car in which he would take her shopping around the city. She got none of those things from Ajit.

Ajay, of course, didn't really hear much of what Barnali was saying to him. But Barnali caught his attention once as she said, "I will find peace only in death in this family," half shouting, half weeping, and walked away toward the kitchen, where she needed to start preparing tea for everyone. Ajay didn't care. Throughout his childhood, Ajay had heard his mother keep repeating those exact words once every few days. Barnali still hadn't found death, nor peace.

The semi-scream seemed to have woken up Ajit too. He let out a scream of his own, "Torturous woman! Everyone in this family longs for the love of a dog for years but cannot have their wish because everyone is living in your fear. And you are simply incapable of loving someone other than yourself. Why did I ever get married to this hideous woman?"

A screaming match ensued between the master bedroom and the kitchen, and it continued for the next fifteen minutes until Barnali came into the living room and called out to everyone, "Tea is served." This was a unique tradition in the Bera family where, for fifteen minutes every morning, Ajit, Barnali, and Ajay sat at the same table every day and no one screamed at another until the tea was over. So, the screaming match ended, and Ajit broke into several stories of how incredible his childhood dachshund, Alfy, was. Ajay listened intently and in exhilaration, while Barnali listened disapprovingly and in contempt.

Arun walked past them and into the bathroom as Barnali asked, "Would you like some tea, Arun?" Arun didn't. Arun was the elder son of the Bera family. Barnali already knew that Arun wouldn't have any tea and hadn't made any for him, but she inquired anyway, out of a habitual courtesy. Arun walked into the bathroom, freshened up, and came back to join them at the table. Arun was excited too.

Arun asked Ajay where he was going to pick up the puppy. Ajay said he would meet the broker, Rudresh, at Manton, which was fifteen minutes from their house, and then they would have to go to Dum Dum, which was literally the other end of the city, to meet the litter of puppies. Arun was excited about the puppy, but had also made it amply clear that Ajay was the one getting it, so all the cleaning-after obligations would fall on him and only him. Nobody disagreed, not even Ajay.

Arun had only just been offered a job in Delhi and was waiting to leave home for the capital at the turn of the new year. Everybody wanted to make sure they were in Arun's good graces before he went off to earn money. The Bera boys continued chatting for ten, maybe fifteen, more minutes, speculating about the puppy that was to arrive, while Barnali sat with them reluctantly at the table. Then they dispersed, and the next hour seemed like any other Sunday morning at the Bera residence. Barnali went into the kitchen and started sorting the condiments she would need for making breakfast and that afternoon's lunch. Ajit went to the market to buy some freshly caught river fish before the good ones got sold out. Nobody really paid attention to what anyone else was actually doing until Ajay called out "I'm leaving" and rushed out of the house before the others could really respond. Ajay left home to and embarked on his long-anticipated journey to Dum Dum to meet the litter that he would choose his puppy from and bring home his favorite new toy!

Ajay met Rudresh in front of the veterinary clinic, at Manton, that had helped connect them with each other. Rudresh arrived five minutes after Ajay had reached the shop. He rode in on his Yamaha RX135 motorcycle and signaled to Ajay to put the shopping bag in his pocket and hop on to the back seat. Ajay did. An hour and five minutes and a bumpy, uncomfortable motorcycle ride later, Rudresh parked the bike in front of an old two-story house in Dum Dum Park. The house was painted light green on the outside but it wasn't one of those plastic paints that give houses their smooth finish. No, it was just a coat of cheap green paint brushed over the plastered cement walls, little patches of the paint coming undone from the concrete at countless places. They got off the motorcycle and took the stairs up, where an old, wrinkly lady met them.

It was a miracle that the flight of stairs didn't come crashing down as Ajay and Rudresh climbed them, one cautious step at a time. The construction looked at least 200 years old and felt even more archaic, thanks to its wobbly structural integrity. With each step, Ajay kept thinking to himself, "Do the residents use an elevator on another side of the building or are they just hoping to fall through one of these days and have the stairwell come crashing down on them to end their misery?"

The lady who greeted the men was only slightly less wrinkled than Taru, Ajay's grandmother, but a tad more shrewd, evident from the twinkle in her eyes. She asked them to wait in an unusually large room with nothing but an unclean sofa placed in the middle of it and went inside. They stood near the sofa for a couple of minutes waiting for the lady to return, but eventually decided it best to sit down, anticipating a longer wait.

As they were about to sit down, a tan dachshund

puppy ran into the room and found the farthest corner from Rudresh and Ajay and sat down. Ajay sprang up with glee as he saw the puppy running into the room, even before his bottom could properly hit the fabric of the sofa seat that he was about to occupy. A wide, unashamed grin and an unfamiliar glow had taken over his face. He ran to the corner of the room and picked up the puppy in his arms, only to find it shaking in fear. He placed it back down on the floor and gently stroked its head a couple of times. The puppy seemed to feel a little relieved, and relieved itself on the floor.

Over the next few minutes, the rest of the puppies from the litter flooded the room. There were six in all. Four of them were chocolate-colored while two were tan. Each one had a different personality. While the first one had found himself the farthest corner of the room to cope with his fear, the third one, another tan one, plonked herself right by the door after entering, but either in a show of attitude or just plain laziness, not fear. A couple of them walked their six, seven-inch frames around the large, empty room, inspecting it like they had moved to a new town and needed to make sure that there was nothing fishy going on. One was fat and seemed like he was used to wresting the lion's share of his mother's milk whenever he had the opportunity. There were only two females among them. A lazy tan one by the door and another chocolate-colored one. This tiny chocolate dachshund was why Ajay had woken up early and traveled all the way across town on a lazy Sunday morning.

He had already agreed to take the chocolate-colored female from the litter; he had paid full money to Rudresh in advance for this puppy because she came cheapest of the six; the visit was, in reality, a mere formality of picking her up and bringing her home.

She looked a little weaker than the rest, her bony ribs perceptible from over her skin. She had a few little white marks on her head. Rudresh assured Ajay that those markings were just drops of her mother's milk that had dried up on her head and will go away with time. She looked sickly but was the sprightliest puppy in the litter. She ran around the room and played with Ajay, some. Rudresh reassured Ajay that she was a healthy puppy, which he said was evident from her playful nature. Ajay picked her up with both hands and asked, "How old is she?"

"Two months and two days today," the old lady replied.

Ajay looked at the pup's eyes and smiled and then took the shopping bag out of his pocket and gently placed her inside. He thanked his host and walked watchfully down those shaky stairs and towards Rudresh's motorcycle.

The journey back home was another ordeal. Ajay hopped on the backseat of the motorcycle but wasn't sure how to hold the puppy stably in the bag while also not losing his own balance. He could secure her over his lap and hope to the higher powers that one of the bumps on the way wouldn't throw him off the moving bike. Or, he could hold on to the back support with one hand for added balance and let the bag with the puppy dangle from the other. It took a minute to find the right seating arrangement so that neither he nor the puppy in his hand got thrown off the moving motorcycle on their journey back home. Even that equilibrium position wasn't ideal, but it had to suffice.

There was over an hour of bustling traffic ahead before Ajay could reach home with the puppy. Fifteen minutes into the ride, it started drizzling. Ajay could feel the puppy trying to adjust positions to minimize her exposure to the rainwater seeping through the surface of the bag. She tried for a couple of minutes, but the bag was made primarily from jute straws, and the pores and openings that allowed her to breathe out also allowed the rain to keep tricking in; it was a case of allowing both or allowing neither.

A little more time passed as they continued their efforts to keep adjusting on the moving motorcycle, and then the puppy started squealing every couple of minutes to let Ajay know of her discomfort. There was not much Ajay could do to control the whims of nature. He requested Rudresh to stop by the roadside and wait a little, under the temporary shade laid out in front of a tea stall. The tarpaulin shade enticed customers to keep stopping by and keep paying for a cup of tea. But Rudresh said there was no point, the rain wouldn't stop anytime soon.

His logic had merit. It was September, nearing the end of monsoon, and extended drizzles during late mornings and afternoons had been the norm for the past several days. But Ajay insisted, and Rudresh eventually obliged. They agreed and stopped at the next tea shop for ten minutes and waited until the drizzle seemed to lighten up a little.

When they made the stop, Rudresh was visibly irate about being delayed for the meeting with his next customer. But the tea was nice, cheap, and piping hot. He calmed down a little after taking a couple of sips. Rudresh was getting drenched as well, up to this point. So, the tea must've come as a welcome respite for him too. Ajay didn't have any tea as he was completely focused on protecting his new puppy, curled up inside the jute bag dangling from his hand, from the evil gaze of curious onlookers that surrounded him. By the time Rudresh finished his cup of tea, the weather seemed to ease up a little as well. Rudresh determined it best to get back on their way now, before the drizzle came back any stronger, or worse, turned into a downpour. They were only halfway home, yet.

Ajay and the puppy hopped back on to the back seat of the motorcycle as Rudresh vroomed away. Ajay could feel the puppy shaking in the bag but she had stopped the squealing. She needed some warmth. Ajay requested Rudresh to stop by the wayside again, but only for a moment this time. Rudresh didn't object. Ajay picked the wet little puppy out of the bag and slid her inside his t-shirt. He thought it would give her some warmth. It seemed to work too; it stopped the shaking for a little while. And they continued for another half an hour until Rudresh dropped him off at the vet clinic in Manton, where they had met earlier in the morning.

Ajay had to take a shared auto-rickshaw back home from there. The first one refused to let him board with the puppy. The second one also denied him a ride because another passenger wasn't comfortable sitting next to a dog. A very faint drizzle had returned by then. Ajay decided that it would be best to take her out of his shirt and put her back in the bag that he was carrying, out of the sight of people, and boarded the third rickshaw without informing anyone of the guest he was hiding in his bag. For most of the ride, the puppy hardly moved or even made a sound. It was shivering a little when Ajay had first boarded the vehicle and placed the bag on the floorboard between his two legs, but it wasn't so much that the passenger next to him would take notice. Once the rickshaw started moving, she stopped shaking after a minute or two. There were no squeals. The puppy just sat still inside the bag. For a passing moment, the worst had crossed Ajay's mind, but mostly, he was thankful that he wouldn't have to get the pup drenched in the rain any longer, and wouldn't have to walk the rest of the way back home.

Just a couple of minutes before Ajay was supposed to get down from the rickshaw, she let out another little squeal. The other passengers got curious. Ajay didn't care if he was thrown out of the vehicle now, it was close enough for him to walk home and the rain had stopped completely. But nobody objected to her presence. The old man seated next to Ajay seemed quite excited at catching a glimpse of her in the bag and put his hand through to stroke her damp coat a little. He told Ajay to make sure to dry her with a towel as soon as they reached home. "I will," said Ajay.

The rickshaw driver turned and asked, "How old is it?"

"Two months," said Ajay.

"Take good care, their immunity is deficient at such a young age," he advised.

Ajay nodded and then asked the driver to stop and let him out. They had arrived at the junction of the lane where Ajay lived and had to walk it from there.

He let the shopping bag dangle from one hand, with the puppy inside, and walked home. He didn't want any of his neighbors to take notice of the puppy and get curious. He just wanted to reach his home!

WHAT'S IN A NAME

Ajay saw the main gate unlocked and walked himself in without any shenanigans. He marched into his grandmother Taru's room, took the puppy out of the bag, and placed her on the bed by Taru's feet. The puppy just sat there still and didn't make the slightest noise. Taru hadn't noticed any of this while she rested on the bed with her eyes closed, until her left foot touched the pup's soft, wet skin and she let out a loud shriek, "Aaaaaaah!"

The shriek got everyone's attention and the Beras all rushed to Taru's aid, only to find her and Ajay laughing out loud together while Taru stroked the back of the little puppy sitting next to her. The mood changed immediately. Nobody was mad at Ajay for almost giving his grandmother her fifth heart attack. Arun moved in close to the bed and started stroking the puppy's back, as Taru doing. Barnali stood at the entrance of the room, half inside-half outside, and looked on. She was angry that Ajay had indeed brought a puppy home despite her reservations. But it was a little puppy, wet and scared. Even Barnali couldn't bring herself to shout at the poor thing. But all the commotion had got the puppy shivering again.

Ajay brought a dry towel into the room and started wiping the rainwater off the wee thing. Ajit asked for someone to switch off the fan so that the pup didn't catch a cold. Arun did.

"You couldn't wait until the rain had subsided before bringing her out in the open?" Ajit quipped at Ajay. Ajay didn't explain himself, just continued trying to dry off the little pup. Ajit wasn't happy to see how sickly and weak the poor thing looked. Ajay explained that she was the liveliest pup of the litter when he met her and how Rudresh assured him that the puppy was healthy. He also explained to Ajit that the little white spots on her head were mere drops of her mother's acidic milk that had fallen on her head and dried into the skin. Ajit wasn't convinced. He said she would be lucky to survive to be old enough to have babies of her own.

Once her skin was fully dry and she had stopped

shivering, Ajay placed her on the floor. She stood there for a few seconds, surrounded by the gigantic humans who surrounded her, and then finally gave in to the demands of her wee bladder and peed on the floor.

Barnali couldn't hold it in anymore. "You are cleaning that," she shouted at Ajit. Ajit, in turn, shouted back, "Why me? Ajay will do it. It is his dog." Ajay went into the bathroom and brought out a discarded piece of cloth and proceeded to wipe the floor with it. Then he went back into the bathroom to wash the piece of fabric and drop it off in a corner. He came back out with a bottle of phenyl and sprinkled a few drops over the soiled area.

The puppy had taken two steps away from the area and stood there, trembling in fear and watching Ajay clean up. As Ajay kept the bottle of phenyl back, she tiptoed her way under the bed and sat down. The trembling didn't stop. She had perhaps hoped to find a shelter to hide from the crowd of the large creatures surrounding her, but the tall legs under Taru's 19th-century pinewood bed weren't ideal for closing off any views. Everyone kept staring at her from different spots in the room while Ajay eventually reached under the bed, picked her up in his arms, and held her close to his chest. She continued to shiver in his arms, but she also seemed to know that Ajay wouldn't hurt her.

This was the first time all of them got a proper look at her shiny, smooth, brown coat. "Brownie!" said Taru, "we should call her Brownie!"

Ajit looked at her and said, "Alfy, Ma. This is our Alfy returned in a new look." Ajit sounded like a thrilled young boy who had just seen a beautiful girl that tickled his hormones as he spoke to his mother about the dachshund that just walked into his life. "What about Chocolate?" inquired Barnali, hesitant still. Arun rejected both Brownie and Chocolate. Arun told them that this was a member of their family. She should have an intriguing name, not how every dog on the street is named after the color of their skin. "Bully," said Ajay, "the first of Bully and Bruno.

"When Ma sent back Silky so many years ago, I knew I would get two dogs one day. The first one would be a German Shepherd named Bully and the second one would be a Labrador named Bruno. She is not a German Shepherd, but she is our first dog and I want our first dog to be called Bully."

Nobody objected. Silky was the name of the Spitz pup that Ajit's colleague had offered to gift them years ago, but Barnali had refused. Ajay had cried his eyes out that afternoon after Ajit's colleague took Silky back with him after fifteen minutes of playtime. Ajay was eight then; and he was twenty now when he replaced Silky with Bully, in his heart. Ajay had earned this name.

Bully would go on to be called several names in her lifetime – Bully, Bulldog, Bullfrog, Bull-Bull by different members of the Bera family. But as the days passed them by, her name kept getting shortened just a little more each time. The final nickname that stuck was Ajay's doing as well. Ajay imagined that whenever any of the Beras would want Bully to stop whatever she was doing in another room and come join them, they would let out the long-drawn yet endearing call of 'Bu...' And 'Bu' would come running into the room within seconds, expecting to be pampered with treats and toys and a share of whatever it is that the family was eating.

ALL GOOD THINGS MUST END

Bully had chosen not to come out from under Taru's bed the previous evening, and seeing how she'd start shaking in fear when anyone went near, no one pulled her out either. Before the family had dispersed, Taru had tried calling out to her several times for a good half an hour. A few times, Bu gathered some courage to shakily walk up to the edge of the bed. As she neared the edge, all of them started cheering and egging her on, which seemed to have quite the opposite effect of what was intended. Bully would get shaken further by all the unfamiliar noises and rush back under the bed. They all comprehended this but none of them stopped cheering, they couldn't help themselves – there was too much adrenaline, too much oxytocin. After half an hour, Taru realized the futility of her efforts in that environment and stopped calling out to Bully anymore.

Arun had been hoping against hope that Bully would eventually realize that this was a family of friendlies and that she had nothing to be afraid of. She didn't. One time, Arun had tried reaching his hands under the bed to escort her out to the open, where all of her new family stood. As soon as his hands touched her skin, the vibrations from her soft, damp skin almost jolted him away like a strike of lightning would. The poor thing was still trembling in fear.

Ajay had also tried reaching in to pull her out from under the bed. He was more persistent than Arun was. He didn't give up after the first attempt. In fact, on the third attempt, Ajay actually pulled Bu out from under the bed and cradled her up in his arms. The trembling seemed to reduce as well after she spent a few seconds in Ajay's arms. Perhaps, Bu eventually realized that this was a safe place. As her nerves seemed to settle down a little, Ajay placed her down on the floor again. Once Bu stopped shaking, he tried playing with her a little. She responded, initially, but then suddenly she stopped and stood still in the middle of the room. A few seconds and she started shaking again and made her way back under the bed.

"They can smell fear and dislike! You will never let anyone feel welcome." Ajit looked at Barnali and quipped. Barnali made her way out of the room after that comment. But she was used to such remarks from Ajit after all these years. Arun deduced that his mother was simply bored by how uneventful and anticlimactic the last hour had been, and it led her to leave the room.

Ajit did not try to pull Bu out from under the bed again. He simply brought in an old rug and placed it under the bed lest Bu caught a cold during the night. He too left after positioning the rug near the far corner under the bed and after watching Bu walk onto it and sit down. Arun left soon after his father did. Ajay stayed back and chatted with his grandmother for some more time.

Ajay liked spending time with Taru but didn't do it as often as she'd have desired. After some time, Barnali called out to everyone informing them that food was served. Taru's maid, who was sitting in the separate kitchen that was used only to cook food for Taru all this while, informed Taru that her food was ready too and proceeded to set up a portable dining table by the side of the bed where Taru could eat. Ajay got up to go find his own dinner in the dining room. With that, they had all said good night and left Bully in Taru's company as they both struggled to stomach some food before they went to bed.

Ajay woke up early again, at the break of dawn, the next day. He was excited about the fun he would inarguably start having with Bully now that she'd spent a night at her new home. Ajay must have woken up with a rare smile on his face with the thought of an undying friendship that he believed was currently gestating, but it was wiped clean within the first few steps he took after getting out of bed. Barnali was lying in wait.

"I had made it very clear that whoever brings the dog home will be responsible for cleaning after it." Ajay could hear Barnali from his room and knew instantaneously what this was about. It was strange not hearing Ajit retort as Barnali kept on shouting through a one-sided fight. Ajay was fearful of the wrath that awaited him as soon as he stepped out of his room but he was already willing to do whatever cleaning he needed to do. Ajay took a deep breath and walked out of his room and made his way toward Taru's.

"Yes, go! Go live in the land of urine and feces. This is what you wanted anyway," Barnali screamed at Ajay.

"It's okay! I am cleaning it; you don't have to worry." Ajay was sincere, but the passive-aggressive tone of his voice didn't sit well with either of his parents.

"I don't want to see any fecal matter lying on the floor in this house even for one second. The consequences will be dire if I have to talk about this ever again. I am telling you right now." Barnali's warning was unambiguous and directed at both Ajit and Ajay. Ajit didn't like that.

"Don't look at me, look at your son. It is his stupid dog!"

His father wanted to get the dog as much as Ajay did, but this was not the time to point fingers. Ajay was about to be on his way, but Barnali retorted, "How does a young boy have the power to enforce his decision in a household? Of course, he couldn't do anything if his selfish father didn't support him. Everyone's wish in this house is important except for the person that takes care of everyone. The only thing I ever wanted was to not be married into a house with a dog. Not one person in this family has ever done one thing for me in the last twenty-five years, except find new ways to torture me every day."

Once again, a lot of the claims and remarks felt tweaked to Barnali's own convenience, but this wasn't the time for pointing fingers.

"Oh, enough! The boy said he was going to clean everything, no one else has to." Taru chimed in with her own scream from the other room. "It is me who is having to live amid all the feces in this room. Why are people who have no role to play and no smells to endure getting agitated over this?"

Ajay proceeded to his grandmother's room to get on with his cleaning rituals while Taru continued screaming at Barnali from afar. "A good-for-nothing woman is leeching off my son for twenty-five years, and she feels no one has done anything for her. In my time, I would have been driven out of the house by my neck if I was as worthless as this woman. And then, my husband would have married another woman into this family."

Ajay did not say anything, but he couldn't have liked hearing all this. A few years ago, Arun would have torn into Taru for those statements, but now he only had to keep his mouth shut for mere months before he could leave this agony behind and go build his career in the capital city. Arun checked his instincts, shut the door to his room, put on the earphones, and cranked the music up to as loud as he could. The voices in the house were louder, still. Barnali had made her way to just outside the door to Taru's room.

"I wonder why your husband never drove you out. You were definitely not worth keeping around. Your husband was a good man, maybe that is why he couldn't treat you as badly as you must have treated him. After living a life with you, no wonder that he died as early as he did."

Ajay had mopped off all the urine spots and the one lump of food that Bu had thrown up already and moved on to cleaning the shit piles from the corner of the room. He stopped cleaning the floor and looked up at Barnali, exasperated, "Ma!"

Taru couldn't respond. She must've wanted to scream back at Barnali but her voice didn't seem to give her any help. Some words did come out of her mouth, but they sounded like complete gibberish as the volume got entirely choked out of several syllables.

"Barnali!" Ajit rushed in and yanked her away by the wrist of her right hand. It made Barnali lose her footing and thereby, her balance. Her elbow hit hard on the edge of the door to the living room, which was diagonally across from Taru's room. The blue paint was chipped off from the door clamp, which was the greatest point of impact. It hurt and the pain was severe for the first couple of minutes. However, hitting that edge had also broken her fall, which could otherwise have caused her surgically replaced hip to come undone again. Everyone had a droplet or two of tears forming around their eyes, reasons completely different from each other. Arun couldn't have imagined Ajay's eyes not moistening a little either, but Taru had told him later that day that Ajay didn't shed a drop of tear until Ajit's final quip at him.

"You are responsible for my mother going through this trauma. And you did nothing to stop this nonsense. Don't you dare interfere if I lose it one day and leave your mother for someone better; even the maid would be better than her." Ajay had had stood witness to several other instances of Ajit not caring about Barnali's physical wellbeing prior to this. He broke, perhaps, because he realized that what Ajit considered an impediment to Barnali's wellbeing was likely much worse than what he had imagined in his mind.

Ajay and Arun had often wondered why their father behaved the way he did. He was inexplicably angry at the entire world but had to keep his mouth shut and head down and continue walking his path. But his bottled-up fit of rage would come uncorked at home every second or third day because the pressure inside the cooker had reached its tipping point and it needed a release. Arun attributed his father's bitterness to the prosthetic left leg that he had to make do with. Ajit had lost his left leg to severe burns while escaping from a tragic house fire the year before he got married. The boys understood that Ajit lived in silent agony all the time so they tried to give their father a pass most on most counts of misdemeanor. Arun had caught Ajit staring blankly at the television screen late on a couple of nights as an army of silent tears kept marching down his eyes. Ajit didn't notice that Arun had seen him in his vulnerable moments and Arun never could bring himself to ask his usually domineering father what was wrong.

Bu kept shaking under the bed through all the unrest but no one paid attention, not even Ajay. For a moment, Bu tried walking toward Ajay from under the bed hoping, perhaps, that he would pick her up in his arms again, and she could feel safe again amid this domestic warfare. But Ajay was bubbling with anger as well. But he had zipped his lips and clasped the mop as tightly as he could in his hands to ensure he didn't do anything to make this worse. Unfortunately, it also meant he had allowed no reasonable outlet to his anger. So, when Bu walked toward him, in his mind, she was the root cause of this misery and he swung his right arm through the air in one flashing motion. He missed her, thankfully. But this led to Bu getting frightened out of her wits, running back to the rug, and continuing to shudder. And now, she didn't even have that one place in the house where she thought that she would feel safe.

PEOPLE SAY THINGS

The fight in the morning was as bad as it could have gotten without Ajit demonstrating what his version of not caring about Barnali's wellbeing looked like. But the good thing was that once it ended, no one spoke a word. Even Arun couldn't remember the last time that the Bera house felt this silent. Their grandfather's funeral several years ago went without anyone raising the voices enough to be noticed, but the murmurs of a hundred people in a house wouldn't have made it seem silent. But that morning's silence was deafening because of all the thoughts ringing out as loudly as they could in each of their heads. It was a strange calm, the calm after the storm, but the warnings of turbulence were still as much in force as they were when Ajay had woken up that morning. The Beras needed some external forces to pacify their emotions. The Ranas, fortunately, were just the guests that the Bera family needed that morning.

The Ranas and the Beras were family friends since before Ajay was born; since Ajit first started building the house that they lived in. Ajit Bera and Mohit Rana had built their houses together, struggled together as they gradually welcomed other families into a once desolate mass of land, and helped build a thriving community together. The Ranas had a bigger house than the Beras and their joint family of five brothers lived there. Mohit was the eldest among his brothers. Only he and the brother immediately next to him were married when he and Ajit had started constructing their houses. Ajit was one of three brothers, himself. Being a part of a band of siblings with no sisters gave Ajit and Mohit a unique motif to build their camaraderie around. Ajanta, Mohit's wife, was loving but strict, a disciplinarian.

Ajay never liked her coming home. It meant he wouldn't be allowed to just sit in his room and brood. He'd have to run errands and participate in conversations. Arun liked being with them. It reminded him that it was possible to be a family, be consistently respectful towards each other, and to resolve differences through openness and communication. Mohit and Ajanta had left to go settle in

Chennai during the 90s. Ajanta had been given a fantastic opportunity to helm a new newspaper that was being launched. They kept coming back home for a month once every year ever since, twice when they could afford to take more vacation days.

It was about an hour of that unsettling calm before a familiar voice started shouting from outside the main gate, "Open the gate, aunty. Is comrade uncle home?" Mohit called Ajit 'comrade uncle' because Ajit once used to believe in several communist ideologies when he was younger.

"Coming," Barnali replied to Mohit's call. Her voice sounded upbeat and optimistic.

"How are you, Mohit?" Taru inquired as the Ranas waited outside the main gate. Ajanta responded, "We are doing okay, aunty. We'll be even better if the house from across ours caused a little less noise pollution in the mornings." Taru joined in on the following chortle with Ajanta, "Only you can break the ice like this, Aju. You should come over more often." Ajanta was blunt but the Bera family had come to appreciate the place of sincerity from which she spoke. She never tried to go out of her way to seem nice and always wanted the Beras to find ways to be happy. They continued to laugh some more until Barnali finally arrived at the gate with a broad smile on her face and let them in.

"Let us go have some tea first. We will meet you on our way out," Mohit told Taru as they made their way into the living room.

"Sit, your comrade uncle is speaking with the plumber," Barnali informed the Ranas. "The flush in the common bathroom has not been working since yesterday, but mister is too busy to call the plumber."

"But, can't you call him yourself, Barnali?" Ajanta asked, trying to ignore the very audible agitation in Ajit's voice as he spoke on the phone in the other room. The unfortunate plumber on the other end of that phone call had to bear the brunt of Ajit's lingering frustration from the fight he had earlier in the morning.

"He will not be satisfied with the work if I get it done," Barnali informed Ajanta. "Arun, Ajay, come and say hi to uncle and aunty."

They came and sat at the dining table, which stood in the middle of the living room. Arun promptly greeted them, "How are you doing, uncle, aunty?

How's your work in Chennai?"

"Your aunty is very busy there," Mohit replied. "She is in her office sixteen hours every day while I come back from the biscuit factory in the evening and make my own tea to have with the same biscuits I get made in the factory! It is the most boring few hours of my day. But your aunty comes home, we eat dinner together, talk about our days for an hour, and go to bed the lovebirds that we like to be when no one is watching." And then Mohit burst into a peal of nervous laughter, worried that he may have given away too much of their personal lives. Ajanta didn't seem particularly interested to extend that conversation thread either.

"So, when are you joining the new company, Arun?" Ajanta asked.

"In a couple of months. I haven't received the exact starting date yet."

"Good, enjoy the free time you get before joining," said Mohit. "How are your studies, Ajay?"

"It's going well."

"This time shouldn't be like last. Your father is working very hard to put you through college, and it puts too much pressure on him if he has to pay one semester's tuitions twice."

Ajit had joined the rest of them at the table by then. Barnali walked away to the kitchen to make breakfast and some tea.

"Ah, let it be. He is an intelligent boy. He will definitely do well this time," Ajanta chimed in. "Anyway, so your mother finally gave in to your demands of getting a dog in the house?"

The change in the conversation turned Ajay's frown upside down! Ajit, too, joined them at the table, "What will I say? Something new gets spoiled in this house every day."

"So, what breed is it?" Mohit, who once had a border collie of his own, was curious and waiting to start drawing parallels from his days with his own dog.

"A dachshund," Arun replied.

"Oh, that tiny sausage-like dog?" Ajanta burst into a bout of laughter as she asked the question. None of the Beras joined in on her laughter so she let it fizzle out quickly.

"A small dog is actually better for a family that mostly stays indoors," said Arun.

"Dachshunds can be very irritating, dumb dogs. They keep barking at everyone for no reason," Mohit added.

"Not at all. I had a dachshund, growing up. I also had a German Shepherd. That dachshund was the most intelligent dog that I have ever seen in my life." Ajit had been very vocal about that when he pushed Ajay to get a dachshund instead of a German Shepherd as well.

Ajay also decided to participate in the conversation, for a change. "Dachshunds are also tremendously vigilant guard dogs. And they have amazing energy."

"Maybe, but it has almost no fur. Their skin looks like that of a mongrel on the street," Ajanta added with twitched, judgmental eyebrows and her characteristic, sarcastic grin. Barnali chimed in as she brought out the now prepared tea and placed the tray on the table, "Actually, if you touch the coat it is extremely smooth and silky. I wish I had hair that silky!"

"Alright, alright! Your dachshund is the most pretty and most intelligent dog in the world," the conceit in Mohit's voice was hard to conceal, "but why are you keeping it in hiding? You don't want us to see it?"

"She has been petrified since yesterday and has not stopped shaking since she arrived. I suppose she is yet to get acclimatized in her new environment. Perhaps also dealing with a bit of separation anxiety after being taken from her mother." Ajit had evidently been thinking about Bu all morning.

"I'll go and get her," said Ajay, and headed back to his grandmother's room once again. It was a good ten minutes before he came back holding Bu in his arms. The light was brighter in the living room and it accentuated all the ribs that her skin was barely draping.

"She looks like she is dying," Mohit exclaimed.

"No, she is healthy. Actually, she was the most active pup of the litter when I went to pick her up yesterday. She was running around the room and playing with me when I engaged. The man at the veterinary clinic who had first told me about her said that the level of activity of a pup is the best indicator of health." The anguish on Ajay's face was unmissable, and he did nothing to hide it either.

"And this imbecile believed him," Ajit shot back.

"The idiot paid full price and bought home the runt of the litter. Now the breeders will sell the other regular puppies at an even higher price."

"Actually, the level of activity is indeed a good indicator of health in pups. When we had that border collie, TomTom, our veterinarian used to say the same thing."

"Don't you want to hold her?" Ajay asked Ajanta.

"Not right now, Ajay. She does look quite ill. I don't want to risk contracting anything – we are traveling to meet my sister tomorrow. She has a toddler at home who I cannot put at risk." The mild glow that had appeared on Ajay's face disappeared in an instant.

"Why don't you take her to a veterinarian today and get her checked out?" Mohit offered his best-intentioned piece of advice to Ajit. "If nothing else, it'll give you the reassurance that there's nothing to worry about."

Ajit brought up the unplanned expenditure that might incur but it was shot down quickly by the Ranas. Ajit never spoke disrespectfully with any outsiders, only his family saw that side of him. Ajit asked Ajay if he had the contact number of the veterinary clinic where he found out about Bu being available for sale. He did. In the next five minutes, the call was placed and Bu had an appointment with the doctor that evening. Robin, the youngest of the Rana brothers, called out to Ajanta from across the street. Breakfast was ready at the Rana residence, and Mohit and Ajanta left to join the rest of their massive family at the dining table.

ISOLATION

Ajit accompanied his two sons to the veterinary clinic in the evening. When the vet finally examined Bu after making them wait for nearly forty minutes, he was stunned. He couldn't believe that such a tiny, young puppy could endure such acute dehydration for two days and not collapse. His first question to the Beras was whether Bu was active. Ajay explained that she was the most energetic pup when he went to pick her up, but she had gone into her own shell since coming home.

"Perhaps she has still not adjusted to her new home," Ajay added.

"Perhaps not, but the shivering is not being caused by the social unfamiliarity. Did she drink any water since you brought her home?"

"No. We gave her a bowl of water and some mashed rice and milk. She didn't touch the water and regurgitated the rice and milk each time she tried having a morsel."

"Hmm..."

"Actually, it was drizzling during our entire trip back home after picking her up yesterday. She might have gotten a little wet. Could she have caught a cold? I dried her up with a towel as soon as we reached home."

The doctor had placed Bu on her side, over his stainless-steel examination table. He kept running his stethoscope up and down her ribs for a couple of minutes as her unusually short breaths got intermittently interrupted by heavy, deep ones. He continued examining her while Ajay continued to share the details of his journey back from Dum Dum the other day. The vet started speaking again only once Ajay was done.

"Well, the getting wet for a long time is definitely not helpful for such a young puppy but what she's got is a case of dehydration. It is not uncommon in dogs. And she's especially vulnerable due to her age. Her immunity is yet to be fully developed. Most puppies on the street end up dead when they get this bad a case of dehydration because they don't receive the intensive care that they need."

Ajay nodded along as the doctor continued speaking, "I'll write up some antibiotics. Make sure you are feeding her these exactly as prescribed. And make sure she's drinking at least two to three pouches of the saline water every day, as I have recommended. It is okay even if she's throwing up some of it. I'll also write up a course of intravenous injections once a day to aid faster recovery. Suman can visit your home once every morning and administer that," he pointed to the coy-looking young woman standing by one corner of the examination table. Suman was his assistant.

Ajit then inquired about the white spots on Bu's head with the vet. He confirmed that those were indeed acidic drops of milk from her mother and nothing to worry about. Ajit let out a sigh of respite after hearing that. Ajit settled the bills at the clinic and prepared to return home.

Suman came back home with the Beras that evening to push the first injection through Bully's tiny veins. Once Suman knew where they lived, she assured them that she would keep returning on her own every evening, starting the next evening.

When Suman came home the next evening, no one came to receive her from the door. Taru's maid had let her in and showed her the door through which to go inside. As Suman entered from the dining/living room door, she would have seen the white goop of regurgitated food by one of the legs of the dining table. As she walked further in, she would have seen the reddish urine rolling down the floor that had almost made its way into the open kitchen. There was a pile of poop in the far corner of the dining room and another pile at the entrance of Ajay's room where Ajit and Ajay were trying to comfort Bu while also trying to push one of those antibiotics that the vet had prescribed down her throat.

Upon entering, Suman was startled by the loud shrieks and screams of Barnali, "I will not live in a house like this. Decide who you want to stay here. The woman who cooks the food that you eat four times a day or the dog who shits and pukes food all over the floor like it is just one huge latrine." While initially startled, Suman also drowned out the noise in her head within a couple of minutes like the rest of the Beras and found her way into Ajay's room.

The fecal matter by the door was from not too long

ago but Suman could also see stains on the floor from the feces inside Ajay's room that he'd done his best to try to clean. It was hard not to feel nauseous around all the stink, stains, and shit around the house but Suman turned out to be quite the professional. She stood in Ajay's room for a minute before Ajit realized she was there. He was a mess.

This was probably the first time Ajay and Arun had seen Ajit weeping like that; bawling, rather. He thought it was all over for Bully. "We tried the entire day to get her to drink the water," bawling still, Ajit pointed to the water bowl by the far end of the bed where he had poured the saline water just like the vet had prescribed. Suman didn't respond. Instead, she took out her cellphone and called the vet, "Sir, that little dachshund that you saw yesterday with the dehydration... I think you should come, visit her once when you close the clinic tonight. She has not touched the saline water, and I think she has been throwing up all day even today." The Beras didn't know what the doctor said from the other side of the phone call, but they heard Suman's words intently.

"Okay...

"So, I will give her the injection now?...

"9.30? Can you make it a little earlier?...

"Drip? Okay...

"Okay. I will send you the address," Suman disconnected the phone and texted the address to the vet. She then asked for a piece of paper, wrote down the details of an intravenous saline drip and the type of syringe to push it with, and asked Ajay to go to the nearest medical shop and get those. She readied the injection that the doctor had already prescribed to Bu the previous day once Ajay left for the pharmacy.

Bully was probably four inches tall from the ground when standing on four legs; five at best. Finding a vein in the left calf, which seemed like no more than an inch of surface area, was a task in itself. On the first day, Bu had squealed a little as Suman pushed the syringe in. But this time, she didn't make any sound at all. She had given in. She lay flat on the floor, on her side, as Suman poked around with the needle to find a vein around the calf of her right hind leg. Ajit watched hopelessly and anxiously. The side of Bully's mouth rested on the floor as well, and a pool of sticky saliva formed around it.

"Wait," said Ajit, and picked Bu up on his lap. He

kept talking to Bu as if she would understand the words coming out of his mouth, consoling her, telling her that the pain will reduce soon. Suman found the vein she was after and pierced it with the sharp object between her fingers as Ajit and Bu both shut their eyes close in internal despair.

It was pushing nine on the clock when Ajay returned, the doctor a couple of steps behind him. The vet had been trying to find their house for a few minutes but couldn't identify it until Ajay saw him wandering about and escorted him inside. He didn't seem bothered by the filth that had overcome the floor in each room through which he passed. The vet spoke with Suman directly.

"You have pushed the IV antibiotics?"

"Yes, sir. Just did."

"Okay, start the drip," he instructed Suman before proceeding to examine Bu himself.

Suman took the syringe off Ajay's hands and asked him to find a place to hang the saline water pouch from the bed. The poking and prodding with the needle started again, this time the shin of Bully's right front leg was in the firing zone. Suman must have pierced the needle in somewhere it wasn't supposed to go. This led to Bu letting out a desperate squeal, which was echoed by one of Ajay's own, and a fainter one from Ajit.

"You leave it, let me find the vein," said the vet, "you go set up the drip." She did. The doctor pinched different parts of the thin skin over Bully's shin until he saw a thin bluish-green line under it, which must have been a vein. He pricked the needle into the vein. Ajay couldn't keep watching anymore. He squeezed his eyes close and a tiny drop of tear squeezed out of the corner of the right one. Bu didn't squeal this time, though. Suman had set up the drip by the time the doctor found the vein he was looking for. Suman had hung the saline pouch from the headboard of Ajay's bed and then handed the connecting tube to the vet to attach to the end of the syringe.

"If she's not eating or drinking, a saline drip is the only option. We'll have to get two pouches in her every day until she's able to feed on her own," said the vet. Ajit nodded.

"Will she recover fully, doctor?" Barnali asked, standing a few steps from the ajar door to Ajay's room. She had been standing at the edge of the door since the doctor entered, but no one had noticed.

"Why do you care? You didn't want a dog in the house, right? Soon, you'll get your wish," Ajit shot back at her.

"I never wanted her to die. Not everyone is like you and your family. You think living in a house this dirty is healthy or hygienic for any of us? There are dogs in so many other houses around us. Do you see those dogs shitting all over in any of those other houses? Being dead would have been nicer than living in this hell, anyway."

"Yes, I would be much happier to see you dead as well. There, I said it." Barnali froze for a moment and then asked the vet if he would like some tea. He declined out of courtesy, and then she left. Ajit went back to ignoring Barnali again and the rest of the people in the room pretended that they were oblivious to the conversation that just took place between the spouses. They all went back to doing what they were doing prior.

Barnali didn't always have the worst of intentions when she spoke but the hostility in the tone of her voice always seemed to bring out the worst in Ajit. Bu had fallen asleep in Ajit's lap by then, so she didn't need to endure the stress of that exchange, thankfully.

Before leaving, the vet told Ajit that it may not be a bad idea to confine Bu to one room until she recovers. He knew that she wouldn't be ready to be potty-trained anytime soon. Suman also left with him after removing the connecting tube of the saline pouch from the syringe that they left stuck into Bully's front leg. Suman would come back the next morning to hang up a new saline pouch and feed the connecting tube into the feeder needle in Bu's leg again. Ajit thought about it a moment after they left and then looked up at Ajay and spoke, "The garage space is empty anyway. I don't think I can buy a car to fill it with before I retire – you boys will have to do that when it's time. We could make her a bed there. Your mother will also not keep screaming endlessly if she doesn't see or smell the feces and urine on the floor all day while doing the chores around the house."

Ajay initially resisted. He said Bully could be confined to his room so he can at least keep her company. But better sense prevailed after a few minutes of back and forth. The garage was the only space where Barnali wouldn't need to enter, so it was only logical to turn that into Bully's room. Ajay told Ajit to leave Bully with him for the night and that he'd help set up the garage for her the next morning. Ajit informed Barnali of the decision, but she just ignored him. She wasn't in the mood to speak to the husband who wanted her dead just yet.

When Ajay woke up the next morning, Bu was still asleep of the floor, by his bedside. He saw that there was another discharge of feces and urine in the room. Bu must have woken up during the night and needed to relieve herself. Ajay didn't even flinch at that sight. He tiptoed out of the room, went to the shared bathroom near the living room, filled up half a bucket of water, put the bottle of phenyl in the pocket of his pajamas, picked up an overused mop, came back into his room, and started cleaning. He didn't realize that Bu had opened her eyes behind him and was watching him clean. Once he was done, he turned around to keep the things back in the bathroom and noticed that Bu was watching him clean her mess. He put the things down, walked over, and petted her forehead for a few seconds, looking blankly into Bully's eyes, without speaking a word.

Suman came home at eight in the morning to reload the drip. The father and sons had moved Bu to the garage by then. It was an empty eight by twelve room with unpolished cement flooring. There was some discarded paper waste dumped in one corner of the room but they made sure that Bully's bed was made far enough away from it. There was an out-of-use water pump in another corner of the garage and Ajay had decided to make Bully's bed by that water pump; perhaps so that it looked less barren around where she'd be lying around all day. The makeshift bed was nothing but an old rug folded over four times to make it thick enough to keep the cold or the heat from the floor at bay when Bu was on it. There was nothing else in the room. The Bera men were all too stressed to even think about placing a toy by the bed to keep their tiny, ailing puppy entertained. To be fair, it didn't seem likely that Bu would be looking for a toy to play with either. Instead, they had set a bowl for water and a bowl for food, which was empty, down of the floor, knowing fully well that she wasn't going to care for either one. But they wanted to hope.

Bu was lying on her belly, chin resting flat on the ground, protruding a little further out of the rug where she lay, when Ajay pulled open the door to let

Suman in. Bully looked up at Suman only by moving her eyes. She didn't so much as lift her chin off the ground where it rested. She just moved her eyes enough to learn who was entering the room and then lowered her gaze back to the ground in front of her. Suman was carrying a metal stand in her hand to hang the saline pouch from. It seemed like Bully knew what was up. She was ready for the pain that was about to ensue, but she trusted that no one in that room meant to hurt her.

THE PLIGHT OF THE HAPLESS

Bu had spent a couple of days in isolation and Ajay believed that she understood the circumstances led to said isolation. The Beras would all take turns to visit her during the day and spend a few minutes entertaining her. She started looking forward to meeting them at various times of the day. Ajit would spend a few minutes with her before leaving for office every morning. If he saw any feces lying around when he visited, he'd take a few extra minutes to dress down to his essentials, clean up the mess, wash his hands and face with soap, and then dress back up and leave for work.

Ajay usually stayed with Bu when Suman visited every morning and every evening to reset the saline drip. He would also clean up any mess on the floor when he visited. That apart, the time in the garage also gave him an opportunity to chat up the young lady who he'd gotten used to keeping company over the past few days for the duration of her ephemeral visits. During the intermittent moments when Suman was too caught up with her responsibilities of healing Bu to pay attention to Ajay's amours, he would just text Ranjana on the phone.

Whenever Ajay visited, Bully would be too sapped of energy to respond to Ajay's petting beyond the initial acknowledgment of looking him in the eye for a second before placing her head back down on the rug she lay on. But that eye contact was like a ray of sunshine for Ajay every day. The big, brown, empathetic eyes almost did not feel like it belonged on a tiny, undernourished body. But every time that those eyes looked up at Ajay, he fell a little bit more in love. He had never known anything like that gaze.

When Ajay was thirteen and he first locked eyes with the girl from the classroom across from his who he'd been watching all day for months prior, the insides of his being went all topsy-turvy with chemicals and emotions. But when Bu locked eyes with him, it was a much stronger feeling that evoked in him, different as well. It made him want to be a kinder person. Unfortunately, that locking of eyes never lasted more than a few seconds. So, Ajay had to find other ways to keep himself amused, and he found the finest of ways possible. Ranjana was Ajay's muse during the early days of college. She didn't know that Ajay had to retake the papers from last semester; bringing up a conversation like that would have caused an aberration in the flirty exchanges that he so enjoyed in their texting. Their relationship worked. Ranjana didn't know that Ajay had flunked last semester and Ajay didn't realize that they were not exclusive. In a twisted way, Ajay and Ranjana seemed like they deserved each other.

Barnali rarely visited Bu in the garage but made sure to check with Ajay, a couple of times every day, if he had cleaned up after her. Ajay would usually confirm that he did, and if not, he would head to the garage to carry out his duties without saying anything back to Barnali. Arun visited once every couple of days. When he visited, he would come out of the garage and inform Ajay if he saw any uncleared piles of shit. If not, Arun would stay an extra minute and stroke his hand through the smooth coat of Bully's fur; long strokes from her forehead to near the small of her back.

On the third, or perhaps, the fourth evening of the

isolation, Ajay walked into the room with Suman to go through their usual motions. Like clockwork, Ajay walked straight up to Bu and started stroking her forehead. But instead of looking up at him, Bu barely lifted her head an inch off the ground and placed back down, displaced half an inch from where it initially lay. Ajay tried talking to her. None of them knew why they felt that way but the Bera family always thought, every once in a while, that their dog could understand their language. And they were all guilty of speaking with Bu, one time or another, like they would speak with each other, only in a nicer tone of voice than usual.

"What happened, Bu? Is the pain more than usual today?" Ajay asked Bu, his voice a little indeterminate, a little offended, a little terrified. Bu did not respond. Suman proceeded to replace the saline pouch hanging from the stand with a new one. Every time Suman started the drip of the saline water, Bu flinched a little before getting acquainted with the flow of the foreign substance into her veins. But today was different. She didn't flinch. Suman noticed that the vein absorbing the saline water had swollen up a little and determined that they'd have to shift the syringe to another vein in her body.

Suman had had to do this once before. That first time, Bu had shrieked and screamed restlessly for a good five minutes as Ajay held her down in his lap and consoled her while Suman pulled the syringe out of her right leg and pricked several tiny holes in several different spots on her hind legs until she found the right spot to stick the ghastly needle in. Bu was inconsolable for a half-hour that day; she would've bitten a finger off Ajay's hand if she had the necessary strength in her body. If anyone else was around, they'd have vouched that Bu was desperately trying to seek out death instead of enduring that pain. Today was different. Suman poked through each limb and even tried finding a vein at the back of Bully's left ear. Bu didn't make any noise. She didn't look up at Ajay even once. She had resigned to her fate. Whatever it was that she needed to endure, she just wanted it to be done with.

Bully looked a little less underfed by this point, thanks to the essential minerals and nutrients being forced into her veins. Yet, Ajay couldn't help but think back to the feisty little puppy he had first met just a few days ago. How she was so much tougher and more resolute than this ailing puppy that lay in front of him. While picking her up from Dum Dum Park, Ajay had thought that this dog was like a tiny little dinosaur, a natural predator that her prey would feel terrorized by, and her family would just observe and admire for her stamina, her sharpness, and her elegance. Bu looked like a very different dog today, one that didn't look forward to life and only wanted whatever was happening to her to just be over.

Suman was done sooner than last time. The drip flowed into a vein near the upper part of the front left leg now. Suman should have appreciated this being much less of a struggle compared to last time but she didn't look like it. Once she was done, she said that she'd come back in an hour to remove the connecting tube from the feeder needle. She assured Ajay that the current pouch of saline water would only get fully consumed right at the time she would return. "Stay with her until I'm back," Suman told Ajay and left. She called up the vet on her way out, "Sir, I think this puppy is giving..." Ajay couldn't hear the rest of it as Suman walked out of the door. She came back in less than an hour, a few injectable medicines in hand and the veterinarian two steps behind her. Ajay was surprised to see the vet with

Suman. He knew in his heart that this could only be the signaling of doom. Barnali, who hadn't visited Bu even once in the garage, walked up to the edge of the garage door in pursuit of the vet. "What is wrong, doctor? Is the dog not getting better?" she asked.

"I haven't seen her yet. Let me examine her first."

Barnali opened the door for him but immediately started retching at the sights around Bu's bed that greeted her from the doorway.

Ajay had picked Bu up on his lap a small distance from the rug that was supposed to be her bed. The bed itself was soaking wet from the urine that Bu couldn't walk further away from the sheets before releasing. Some of Ajay's pajama was also wet with it. It looked like Bu had relieved herself again after finding herself on Ajay's lap. There was a pile of dark yellow stool on the edge of the bed, part of which stained the floor and a more substantial part was pasted onto one corner of that makeshift dog bed. That pile had neither a clear state nor a definite form and was gross enough to drive away anyone else from the house other than perhaps a vet and his helper.

The vet tied his handkerchief around his mouth and nose and walked in, leaving Barnali behind. He got to work with his stethoscope jammed into his ears. After some more examination, he pointed to Ajay to step outside to talk. Barnali came back to the doorway and threw in an old bedsheet toward Ajay's direction. "Don't put her back on that urine-soaked rug," Barnali told Ajay, after having momentarily recovered from her gagging, and went back into the house. Ajay put four folds on the bedsheet and spread it out on a dry area on the floor, placed Bu down on it before stepping out into the corridor to speak with the vet. Suman joined them as well.

"This is not a good sign. Her wanting to recover is a big part of the process of recovery," the vet told Ajay as Ajit returned from work and joined them in that corridor. Ajit wasn't privy to the deterioration in Bu's will to fight her ailment yet. He feared the worst. "What happened to Bully?" Ajit sounded like a little kid who came back from school and found out that his unscholarly sibling had finished off the last piece of chocolate that he was saving to reward himself with at the end of the week.

"She's alive, still, but she looks like she's giving up hope," the vet told Ajit.

"Oh, then? That little thing surviving on injections and stabbed by needles all day, do you really blame her?"

"No, I don't. But those needles and injections are what's keeping her alive so she needs to endure a little more of that, I'm afraid."

"How much more?" an anguished Ajit retorted.

"We can't be sure but she looks a little less scrawny than when I last saw her. That suggests that she's able to absorb some of the nutrients from the drip. That is a good sign."

"Hmm…" the agony on Ajit's face diminished a little upon hearing that statement from the vet.

"We will have to give her a few more injections, though. I've prescribed some antibiotics for the next five days."

"More needles, poor thing! Doctor, I've had two dogs when I was growing up but we never had to put them through this much torment."

"Well, they didn't get acute dehydration when they were two months old, now, did they?"

"No, but still…"

"I am hoping these antibiotics over the next five days will kill off any internal infections. Besides, your brave little dog won't need to be 'stabbed' any more than what she is already enduring. Suman will just push the medicines into the drip, which is already intravenous," the vet smiled a little while informing Ajit. Neither Ajay nor Ajit found it in them to reciprocate that smile.

"Don't worry, she'll get better," said Suman.

Ajit walked the vet out of the house and paid him for his visit just as he was about to leave. It was a strange feeling for Ajay, seeing that. The man who was infuriated if his sons bought a packet of Ramen noodles or a packet of chips as an evening snack didn't show a hint of bother as half of his monthly salary was on its way to being passed off to the veterinarian and his assistant.

The same routine continued over the next few days. Ajit would clean the garage floor once before leaving for work and Ajay would clean it another couple of times during the day. Suman would continue to visit once every morning and once every evening to start the drip and, thereafter, inject the antibiotics to go along with it. From the next day, Bu began to flinch for the first few seconds again when the drip started. Strange as it was, Ajay was relieved and happy to see Bu responding to pain. However, Suman explained that this could also be because the initial absorption of the solution was likely slightly more painful to Bu's veins now, with the addition of the newer antibiotics. Other than that, though, Bu did not show any real signs of regaining her feistiness. If anyone entered that room between the cleaning routines, they'd find three or four pools of reddish urine around Bu's bed; some of it would be trickling down to the street outside from under the iron door of the room once envisioned as a garage for a red Maruti car. There would also be a pile of stool every four hours on a good day, and two or three piles on a bad one. As the days passed, Ajay longed for the few times that he would find the shit-piles on the empty floor, far away from Bully's bed instead of on it. Ajay had to change the bed-sheets that Bu lay on at least once a day. He would also wash any sheet that got soiled and never really complained about it. Ajit also developed a habit of cleaning the floor one last time before going to bed, a couple of hours after he returned from work late in the evenings.

Ajay did not spend much time together with Ajit since he failed those two subjects in college last semester. And the little time that the father and son did have to spend within the same enclosures was usually filled with apathy and awkward silences.

Ajit always felt that his family had no empathy toward him, otherwise they wouldn't have left the task of cleaning the soiled garage floor for him during the little time he'd have at home. Meanwhile, Ajay felt utterly underappreciated for being a responsible pet parent, ensuring that Bully's surroundings are cleaned multiple times each day, and ensuring that Bu's living conditions maintained at least the bare minimum levels of hygiene required, and yet never being recognized for his efforts.

A few days passed like that, and not much changed. One of those afternoons, Ajay was getting ready to complete his second round of scooping feces off the garage floor, but on his way to the garage, he heard Barnali's voice coming from that garage and stopped himself from walking further up. It was a rare moment and Ajay didn't want to interrupt it. He stood at a distance, which he felt was safe enough for doing a little bit of eavesdropping without being seen.

"This needle stuck in you all day must really hurt, right Bu? But you have to get some nutrients in your body. If you don't eat anything, then the doctor has no choice but to feed you through this needle. I will make you some boiled rice and chicken stew once you start eating."

Ajay continued listening and stood still, teary-eyed, in his position until he realized that Barnali hadn't spoken a word in a few seconds. It dawned on him that Barnali must be on her way back so he hurried back to his own room. Barnali returned, cleaned her hands with the old soaps that Ajit had squeeze-glued together to extend their longevity. She took some time washing her hands at the washbasin outside the kitchen and went back to her usual chores. Ajay waited another five minutes before heading back to the garage. He still had to clean the mess that Bu would have created since his last visit that morning. When he entered the garage, there was nothing to clean. There was no pile of shit, no urine, not even the stains that Ajay sometimes couldn't mop off completely from the floor after scooping the feces off it. Bu's bed had already been replaced with a washed bedsheet, the soiled one was hanging from a wire that hung about six feet from the ground and between two walls bordering the width of the room, far enough away from the bed. A stick mop, a bottle of disinfectant, and some old, worn out pieces of cloth lay in one corner of the room. Ajay couldn't believe what had happened, although unsurprisingly, miracles like that did not happen often after that day. But that afternoon was special. A weepy-eyed Ajay petted Bu for a few minutes without having to worry about the cleaning chores. Bu seemed to enjoy the attention again, although she still wasn't really mobile, still. But she had started looking up at Ajay every couple of minutes again, especially if the petting lost a little of its intensity.

When Ajay came out of the garage, he washed his hands and asked Barnali, "Is lunch ready?"

"Yes. Will you eat at the dining table or should I serve you in your room?"

"No, I'll come to the table. You can serve here."

Ajay and Barnali had lunch at the same table after months, that day. Usually, Ajay would use his studies as an excuse to bring his lunch plate to his room and eat while watching pixelated videos of Japanese porn on his phone. Nor Barnali neither Ajay said anything during that lunch, but it was the most perfect afternoon in either of their memory that they had shared together.

Ajit returned home a little earlier than usual that evening. After the afternoon that she had had, Barnali was also in a better frame of mind than usual. She had just finished making *pakoras* to serve with the evening tea when Ajit entered the house.

"Oh perfect," said Ajit. "I was just thinking that I should go up to the food cart up the street and get some *pakoras* to munch on while having the tea this evening."

"Freshen up, I'll serve on the dining table."

Ajit proceeded to the master bedroom to change, freshen up, and come back to the dining table for the snack. The day was turning out to be very pleasantly surprising. Barnali and Ajay sat together for lunch earlier and now it seemed like Ajit and Barnali were willingly about to sit together to share the evening tea and some rare moments of conversation and chitchat. Neither Ajay nor Arun wanted to be a third wheel in this rare moment, so they took their share of the *pakoras* into their respective rooms and listened intently, ears to the walls, for what their parents were chatting about.

"Did you have less work than usual today?" Barnali asked.

"No, but a new fellow joined the office. He just got transferred into our branch today. Young lad, strapping. I showed him some stuff and asked him to take care of filing the earnings data after the showroom closed to customers."

"Oh. That's good. Hopefully, he can help you out with some of your responsibilities from now on."

"Not likely. I'm sure Acharya will assign him to handle the cash, eventually. That's what the fellow did at his previous branch. But I'll take the help while I can still get it."

"By the way, Pinky came home this evening."

"Who's Pinky?"

"She's the tailor who bought that small studio apartment last year, only a few buildings down from ours. She is a single mother putting her daughter through cooking school. Must be difficult for her. Anyway, I gave her some of my old clothes to sew in some new designs and add some finesse. She was giving great discounts."

"Of course, she will. How many clothes did you give her? How much money is she charging? Do you have the slightest idea how hard I have to work to earn every last penny that I do?" Ajay and Arun didn't have to listen intently through the walls of their room any longer. Both Ajit's and Barnali's voices gradually started reaching the volume at which they usually communicated with one another, where at least three neighboring houses could follow the conversation even if they didn't want to.

"Go to hell! This is why I have never complained that you come home late from work every evening. This house becomes a slum as soon as you enter."

"You are the woman who turns this house into a slum. Have you spoken with the ladies who are your neighbors? Their husbands don't earn half as much as I earn and yet their families live comfortably. Those wives know how to save money and where to spend it."

"Yes, everyone else's wife is perfect. Only your wife is an idiot. She may have to walk about draped in tattered clothes but why would you care? My respect and dignity obviously do not mean a fucking thing to you."

"No, it does not. I don't care about your senseless whims. And nobody respects you anyway, tattered clothes or not. Have you considered how much money I am draining to keep that little dog alive?"

"Did I tell you to get that dog? Who wanted the dog? You did. So, you have to pay for it, obviously. You should have thought about the expenses before buying her."

"Ah, enough," Taru finally shouted out from her room. But Barnali and Ajit didn't pay much heed to her plea for at least a few more minutes. "Enough, I said." They stopped shouting after hearing Taru yell out a second time but kept muttering insults at each other under their breaths. One would catch air of what the other one muttered and a screaming match would follow, which would last for another couple of minutes until Taru yelled out something at them again.

THE STRENGTH OF WILL

The days passed and they followed the usual patterns. It was almost a month now that Bu had spent in isolation. But a miracle was awaiting Ajay as he escorted Suman into the garage that morning like every other morning in the past month. Ajay opened the door and saw that Bully was sitting up on her bed, hindlegs stretched out front to near where the paws of her upright front legs rested on the ground. Ajay was overcome with emotion but lacked any capacity for articulation. "Bu..." he called out fondly to his feisty little fighter and she responded with the sweetest little sound that was intended to be something between a bark and a howl but sounded like the cry-laugh noise made by human toddlers. Ajay rushed in to hug her but slowed down, thinking he didn't want to hurt her by accidentally displacing the feeder needle, which was now sticking into one of her hind legs. He sat down next to her and started massaging the fur around her chest. Ajay felt like Bu's coat was almost as silky as it was on the day when he first brought her home, after he had patted her dry with a towel. Arun could hear the jubilant tone in Ajay's voice from his room as he spoke with Suman and decided to join them in the garage without delay. It indeed was a sight for sore eyes, seeing Bully sitting up and enjoying her cuddles after so long. Barnali had also come to stand by the ajar door, hearing all the ruckus. Suman said, "Let me call sir. I think we can take Bully off the saline drip now. She should be able to eat normally now."

The vet visited again that evening after Ajit returned home and confirmed Suman's diagnosis. "Seeing her now and when you had brought her into the clinic is like night and day. Who would believe that this is the same skinny little dog that you had brought in last month? In fact, I think she might get a little chubby pretty soon. Make sure you start giving her some exercise as soon as is able to endure that, physically." Everyone in the room shared nervous little smiles at that analysis by the vet, and then he continued, "But give her liquid foods for a few days. Overboil some white rice, add some water, and serve her that mixture. Don't try to feed her any meats yet. And no processed dog foods." The Beras all nodded along as the vet continued. "I will continue a couple of the medicines but will change them from injections to tablets. You can bury it in the food. Your dog will eat it unknowingly as long as she's eating the food. Also, Suman will keep coming back every couple of days over the next week to make sure that Bully is nursed back to her best health."

Suman disassembled the drip system. Then she pulled out the needle that was piercing Bully's leg. Bu squealed a little as Suman pulled the needle out. Suman covered the needle wound with a ball of cotton and tied a gauze cloth around it. Bu didn't show any signs of discomfort a few minutes after that. Then Suman left, as did the doctor. Barnali came by after an hour with a bowl of overboiled rice like the vet advised. She handed the bowl to Ajay, who had returned with the tablets from the pharmacy by then. Barnali asked him to mix it properly before giving it to Bu. She went into the house and came back again in a minute and placed a filled water bowl by the wall next to Bully's bed. Bu walked up and took a couple of sips of that water as Ajay and Arun both watched in delightful wonder. Ajay mixed the tablets with the rice and placed it next to the water bowl. Bu ate a few morsels and then walked back, gingerly, onto her bed, but without any assistance, and lay down without finishing her food.

Thankfully for the Beras, she didn't regurgitate the little rice that she did eat. Arun asked his mother to serve their dinner at the dining table and informed her that they'd eat on their own time before going to bed. Barnali finished her dinner around ten and she went to bed. Ajit, Ajay, and Arun continued snuggling with Bu for another hour, maybe more, then they each retired to their beds after eating their food at the dinner table, a few minutes apart from each other.

Over the next few days, Barnali made a habit of cooking and serving the boiled rice for Bu twice a day, just like she would cook food for the rest of the family, and refilling Bu's water bowl anytime she noticed that Bu had drunk some of it. She didn't do the cleaning, though. If she found any mess on the garage floor when she went to serve the food, Barnali would call out to Ajay to clean up first and then come back with the food after he was done. Barnali didn't mind cooking and bringing the food for Bu but was annoyed that she'd never finish the portions served. She tried several flavor additions to the rice to get Bu to finish. One day, Barnali would add a little hung curd to the rice, and another day, she would mix the rice together with some mashed potatoes. Alas, nothing seemed to motivate Bully enough to finish all of her food. That didn't mean that there was no improvement. Each day the fecal discharge would move a little further away from the bed and the eating area. There was no urinating on the bed any more. The greeting bark when someone entered the garage was starting to become a pattern. Almost a week passed and aside from not finishing her food, everything about Bu's health was moving in the right direction. Suman assured the Beras that Bu would start finishing the entirety of her meals as she gains more strength and is able to become more active. Until then, Suman advised that Barnali reduce the portion size for the meals a little. Barnali did, but Bu still didn't finish the portions served.

Barnali gave up trying to get Bu to finish the food by the end of that week. On a Sunday afternoon, Barnali stopped trying to wait around and egg Bully on while she ate. She simply placed the plate of over-boiled rice mixed with the mashed potatoes down by Bully's bed, refilled the water bowl, and turned back to return to the kitchen. As Barnali was about to shut the garage door behind her on her way out, she heard that familiar, demanding yet endearing, bark behind her. Barnali turned around and saw Bu looking up expectantly at her. The bowl of rice and mashed potatoes had been emptied already, and Bu wanted more.

Barnali walked back in, picked up the bowl, looked at Bu, and said, "Wait, I'll come back with more." A strange mirthful grin had hijacked the whole of Barnali's face as she left with the emptied bowl of rice in her hands.

FAMILY

Hope is a beautiful thing. It can come upon us like an avalanche if we give it the slimmest inch of space to trickle in. But often, the thing about hope is that it muddles our interpretation of reality. When we get a text in the morning from someone, if we know them only a little, we start to hope that we will now get to know them at a much deeper level and that they will eventually fall in love with us for the people that we are. When our spouse returns home early from work, we start hoping that they wanted to make time for us in their lives. When we land a job, we start hoping that we're about to set off on our wildest and most profligate fantasies. If we have an ailing pet dog who is suddenly able to eat a full bowl of rice and wants more, we start hoping that they're just one tiny step away from running around the house and driving us all crazy with their antics. But when we review the facts, hope, in most cases, show us the most exaggerated and implausible version of our future lives. It is only a minuscule number of situations in real life that we get that which we hope for. And it is in those rare few cases that hope becomes a beautiful, incredible thing. Perhaps the best of all things that exist in the universe.

Once Bu demanded for that second bowl of rice, there was no looking back. Having witnessed her appetite for a couple of days, Arun stopped judging Ajay for comparing Bu to a dinosaur that one time when the brothers were shooting the breeze. Bu's tiny little head could fit in the palm of either of their hands, the pointy nose might have stuck out if a smaller child had offered Bu to rest her chin on the palm of their hand and wrapped their hand around the snout as a form of playful teasing. Ajay did precisely that every once in a while, but he would open his slightly larger hands within seconds to ensure Bu didn't feel any suffocation. The next few days turned out to be rather uneventful, anticlimactic almost. Ajay, Arun, Ajit, Barnali, and Bu, they all got used to the routine fairly quickly. Bu found a spot at the end of the garage, which faced the street outside, to perform all her duties through the day. Ajay and Ajit found an acceptable pattern for cleaning the defecations so as not to put Barnali in a position of catching a glimpse of any of it. Bu started wagging her tail and prancing around a little when any of the Beras entered her garage room. She couldn't stop wagging her tail for a whole minute when all the Beras came to visit her at dinner time for the first time and the Beras couldn't get enough of that event. Arun decided to buy a digital camera the next month to document everything Bu would do to entertain the Beras. As some more time passed, she was able to indulge in a bit of wrestling as well.

When everything started to fall in place, Ajit declared, "She will sleep with me at night, starting today." Ajay was the first to voice taking exception to the statement, "No, she will sleep with me. Right, Bu?" Ajay looked at Bu as if expecting her to vote on the matter and Bu looked back up at Ajay and simply let out her archetypal bark, which the Beras had by now grown as familiar with as they had become fond of. There was a battle of logic that followed but Ajay conceded defeat without putting up a real fight. The fight between Ajit and Barnali, thereafter, was a much more hard-fought bout.

"Under no circumstances am I sleeping with a dog on my bed," said Barnali.

"You don't have to sleep on the bed then. I will sleep with Bully. You go make yourself a bed on the old sofa in the living room."

"Why should I? You want to sleep with the dog. Then you figure a way to achieve that. That dog is not getting up on my bed."

"That is not your bed. I bring the money home so that we can continue to have that bed in the house."

"This bed was a wedding gift from my parents. Only I have a real right to sleep on it."

"I don't care. This is my house and you are not allowed in my house if you have a problem with me sleeping with my dog."

Barnali didn't concede defeat, but Ajit declared himself the victor in that war of words not too long after. Barnali didn't win many of the fights she had with Ajit. Whenever she looked like she could be getting the upper hand, Ajit would play his trump card – he was the sole breadwinner of the family. Barnali was angry, disturbed, upset, and she spent half the night lying awake on her side of the bed and muttering indecencies under her breath on one edge of the ancient bed her parents had endowed her with when she married into the Bera family.

But Bully slept peacefully on the bed throughout the night between Barnali and Ajit, positioned in such a way that she could feel the touch from them both. This must have been quite a welcome change for Bully, compared to sleeping on folded bedsheets laid down over a cold floor.

Barnali had later claimed that she wasn't able to fall asleep until three in the morning because of Bu being on the bed but the rest of the family only noticed her discomfort when she woke up in a wild fit of rage even before the clock struck five. The loudness of her screams, directed at Ajit, caused both Ajay and Arun to also wake up, startled. It wasn't a surprise that Taru couldn't sleep through the screaming either. It was still yet to hit five on the clock in the morning, but Taru and Barnali were already at it from across the rooms.

"Barnali, you will give me another heart attack! Do you really want me to drop dead in your house?" Taru's voice sounded as horrified as it was incensed. Who could blame her?

"Yes, drop dead. That is the only way I will ever get any peace in this house."

"Why don't you die instead? So many people can

find peace instead of just you!"

"Of course, that is the plan you mother and son are hatching as you both sit in your room whispering little strategies to each other every evening. Did you think that I don't know?"

Ajit could snore through earthquakes. The Bera boys got that quality from him. But he finally woke up when the exchanges between his wife and his mother had escalated to death threats and conspiracies. That he could sleep through the last five minutes of that screaming match was admirable in its own right.

"Ah, what is wrong? Why are you both shouting in the middle of the night?"

"It is not night, it is morning. But of course, you do not know that. What do you really do outside of your office? I have to even serve tea in bed for this sap." Five in the morning was probably the only time of day when Barnali could get a real upper hand in a fight with her husband.

"Enough! Why are you shouting?"

"Don't you have eyes? Can't you see? Can you not even feel anything below your feet?"

When Ajit looked down, he saw Bully sat on the edge of the bed just below his feet. Her two front paws were stretched marginally over the ledge of the bed and she was taking small, restless steps back and forth with her hind legs. Bu was trying to jump off the bed to the floor but the height of that jump must have seemed like a little too much to her. She had wet the bed before she could muster the courage to jump down to the floor from it. In one swift motion, Ajit picked Bu up from the edge of the bed and placed her on the floor below. There was enough snap in the motion of his hands to make it seem like he threw Bu away but not enough thrust for it to harm her in any way. Bu looked up, scared, at Ajit for a brief moment before scampering away to that garage room that was her safe haven until last night.

"Why are you screaming at my mother? What will she do? Where is your son? Didn't he say that he will take all responsibility for the dog? That little puppy will obviously have a small, weak bladder. It is only natural that she will need to relieve herself early in the morning? Does Ajay even know that he has to take her to pee and poop in the morning every day? That illiterate scoundrel probably doesn't even know that I've had to clean feces in the garage every morning so far before leaving for office."

When Ajit was angry, Ajay would often become Barnali's son instead of both of theirs. And while Barnali would have given him a mouthful if Ajay had been in her sight at that moment, she rarely ever said anything to aggravate Ajit's wrath, when it was directed toward her sons. That morning was no different. The argument found an organic fizzling out point with no resolution once Barnali stopped talking back. She left the argument at, "I don't care. I am not washing this bedsheet." She pointed to the wet corner of the bed as she said that, and Ajit didn't say anything back after that either.

Bu had taken this opportunity to go and take a dump in that one corner of the garage that nobody had ever reprimanded her for using as a lavatory. When she was done, she initially intended to go back to the master bedroom. But as Bu stood near the doorway and observed while the screaming continued, she decided it best to find herself a safer nook. She ran into the dining room and sped under the old sofa by the damaged yellow wall. She thought that it wouldn't be easy for the strange, giant creatures, who couldn't seem to decide whether they loved her or unequivocally despised her, to drag her out from under there. She wasn't wrong. As they all hesitantly made their way into the dining room for the morning tea routine, Arun noticed Bully's big brown eyes looking up at them from under the sofa and gleaming like Smeagol's did when he caught a glimpse of the *ring* in Ajay's favorite epic fantasy. Arun pointed it out to the others but no one seemed to be in a mood to entertain his idiosyncratic thought. Bu stayed in hiding under the sofa as Barnali kept hurling accusations at Ajit and Ajit kept bouncing those off to Ajay. Ajay wanted out of there, so he figured he could follow through on Arun's finding of Bu's hideaway. After considerable persuasion and coercion, he lured Bu out from under the sofa, cradled her up in his arms, and headed to the terrace.

In the next few minutes, the screaming reduced and it seemed like Bu and Ajay had also not let their traumatic experiences from earlier thwart their enthusiasm. Arun could hear the footsteps echo down the ceiling as Ajay and Bu ran around the terrace playing 'catch me if you can!' After a few minutes, the echoes of footsteps running around the terrace also softened. Ajay had tired himself out, but Bu continued trotting around the terrace for some more time. This was her first visit to the terrace and she seemed to enjoy the apparent freedom of a larger open space. Once she stopped running, she walked up to a drainage hole that connected to the drainage system of the house and proceeded to pee there. Ajay stood still and watched. Once she was done doing her business, Bu looked up at Ajay again.

"That's my Bu! You're such a smart girl." Ajay rushed toward her with a big grin on his face, cradled her up in his arms again, without caring for the fact that a last, unreleased, drop or two of urine had now been leaked onto the shirt he was wearing. Instead, he continued showering verbal praises and adulations on Bu. As Ajay turned around to go back down to the dining room, he saw Ajit, Barnali, and Arun, standing at the door of the terrace. All of them were grinning ear to ear as well. Neither Ajay nor the rest of the Bera family could wipe the smiles off their faces for the next few minutes; not that they wanted to smile, but they couldn't help themselves.

"You know that you're supposed to pee near the drainage hole, Bu?" Arun said to her. "You are such an incredibly smart little girl, aren't you?"

Ajit chimed in as Arun continued smiling, "Of

course, she is! She is the smartest girl in the house!" Everyone knew that statement was a jab at Barnali but, in that moment, no one cared, not even Barnali herself. Ajit continued, "Did you get scared because I threw you off the bed, Bu? I'm so sorry. I didn't mean to. I was just disturbed because I just woke up and your Ma was already at my throat."

Barnali must've been thinking to herself, "If only I had gotten such apologies after our fights, our relationship would have been so different." Barnali didn't say it out loud, though. She looked at Bu and spoke through a rare, radiant smile, "You have expelled everything in your system since morning now, you little monster. You must be famished. Let us all go back down now. We will have breakfast together."

With that, Barnali turned around and went back down to serve breakfast. The rest of them followed after her. As Barnali prepared *parathas* in the kitchen, the rest of them made themselves comfortable at the dining table. Before sitting down on his chair, Ajay put Bu down on the floor by him. As they all waited, Bu kept trying to climb up Ajay's leg to join them at the table.

"No.

"No, Bu.

"Sit."

Ajay resisted a few times but seeing that little dachshund who stood barely a few inches off the ground trying to climb up to one of the dining chairs was simply too adorable to resist, beyond a point. It took Ajay all of thirty seconds to succumb to the pleas. He picked Bu up and sat her down atop the chair next to his own. When Barnali walked up to the table with the tray of *parathas* in her hands and saw Bully sat at the table, Ajay expected the air around them to get hard to breathe again. It didn't.

"You will eat at the dining table? Are you also a human being like us? Why don't you walk on two legs like us then?" Barnali let out playful little smirks as she directed those questions at Bu. Barnali had brought a separate bowl of wet food for Bu earlier and but she abandoned that in the center of the dining table, a little too far from where Bu was sitting. "Will you be able to eat these parathas?" Barnali asked Bu. Arun wondered in his head when the last time was that the Bera family had a breakfast gathering this amicable and pleasurable. They all started eating the *parathas*. Ajay kept tearing off tiny bites off his own *parathas* and feeding them to Bu. She must have eaten half a stuffed *paratha* before she stopped.

"Full already, you tiny dinosaur?" As rhetorical as the question was, Ajay enjoyed being able to call Bu a 'tiny dinosaur' in front of the rest of the family as it seemed to bother Ajit, who found that nickname indecorous to Bu. Ajay laughed out loud as his father shared his indignation over the taunt. But with that half a stuffed *paratha*, Bully's breakfast was done. "Okay, time for you to get off from the chair now," Barnali said in jest. But Ajay didn't want to take any chances. All he heard was that his mother, who seemed to be in a rare joyful mood, wanted Bu off the dining chair now. Ajay didn't want to take any chances.

Ajay placed Bu back down on the floor, and the urine came crashing down and hit the granite flooring like a waterfall from a very high mountain or like a downpour of acid rain on drought-hit crops of a malnourished farmer!

Barnali wanted to get furious, but couldn't bring herself to start screaming. Instead, she burst into maniacal laughter acknowledging the incorrigibility of their new family member. There was nothing they could do anymore.

Bully had already become a member of the Bera family now. And the unforgettable adventures of SuperBu was just about to begin.

***

Please turn over and read the next few pages for some useful information.

THANK YOU FOR READING...

Thank you for reading. If you enjoyed this book, consider leaving a review on Amazon or Goodreads to help your friends and family, as well as other readers like yourself, discover the book.

You can give this book a shoutout on social media. Use the hashtag - **#superbu** and tag my social media accounts.

By the way, now that Bully has fully regained her health, SuperBu will be back soon for her next adventure. Keep an eye out for the next novella in this series.

Or better yet, you can join the tribe on my website.

www.dkiswriting.com

You can also follow me on social media:

Amazon - author.to/dkiswriting

Instagram - *@dkiswriting*

Facebook - *@dekanjilal*

LinkedIn – *Debarshi Kanjilal*

And if you have the ability to care for one and room in your heart, consider adopting a stray animal. The love they give is no less than that of commercially-bred pets.

THE BUZOLAND PROJECT

As I have already told you, this book is inspired by the story of a little brown dachshund that my family and I once had. And I want to try to do some good in her name, if I can. The Buzoland project is a dream I have long nurtured to that end.

Think of a dog shelter near you. When I think of the ones around me, I visualize one of two things. I see old dogs trapped in tiny cages, who were abandoned by their families due to old age, illness, or some other excuse. I'm not judging these families. I found myself in that same scenario once not too long ago. Alternately, I see stray dogs being packed together in small spaces, living out their lives with hearts full of love yet not knowing what it is to be a pampered pet.

The Buzoland project is my dream to offer a small piece of land where some of these dogs will find a home, not a shelter, be loved like a member of the family, and live life like the pampered pets that they deserve to be.

I intend to use a significant portion of the proceeds from the sale of the SUPERBU books to fund this dream project. So, when you buy a copy of this book, you will not just be buying a couple of hours of reading an incredible story, you will also be investing in the betterment of the lives of a few dogs who are waiting for someone to swoop in and unleash the superpower of their love and kindness.

So, again, thank you for reading and thank you for playing a part in, one day, finding a dog a loving home.

ABOUT THE AUTHOR

Debarshi Kanjilal

Debarshi Kanjilal (DK) is an urban fiction writer based out of Bangalore, India. His debut novella, Based on Lies, was touted as a gripping psychological thriller by several reputable reviewers. In 2020, DK returns with his latest novella, SuperBu: Homecoming, an emotional journey of a family and their dog.

Debarshi ran the 'God of Absurdity' blog from 2012 to 2015, which published humorous anecdotes and reflection pieces. He is also an accomplished learning experience design professional who has helped shape adult learning strategy for some of the most well-known organizations in the world.

Made in the USA
Middletown, DE
06 September 2020